OZZIE &
PRINCE ZEBEDEE

Gela Kalaitzidis

FLAMINGO
BOOKS

Ozzie the Dragon and
Prince Zebedee were
the best of friends.
And like all best friends,
they did everything together.

Prince Zebedee liked to invite Ozzie over for tea.

Ozzie liked to take Prince Zebedee to play in the park.

And the two friends made
beautiful music together.

At night they kept each other's feet warm.
They were the best of friends.

Most times.

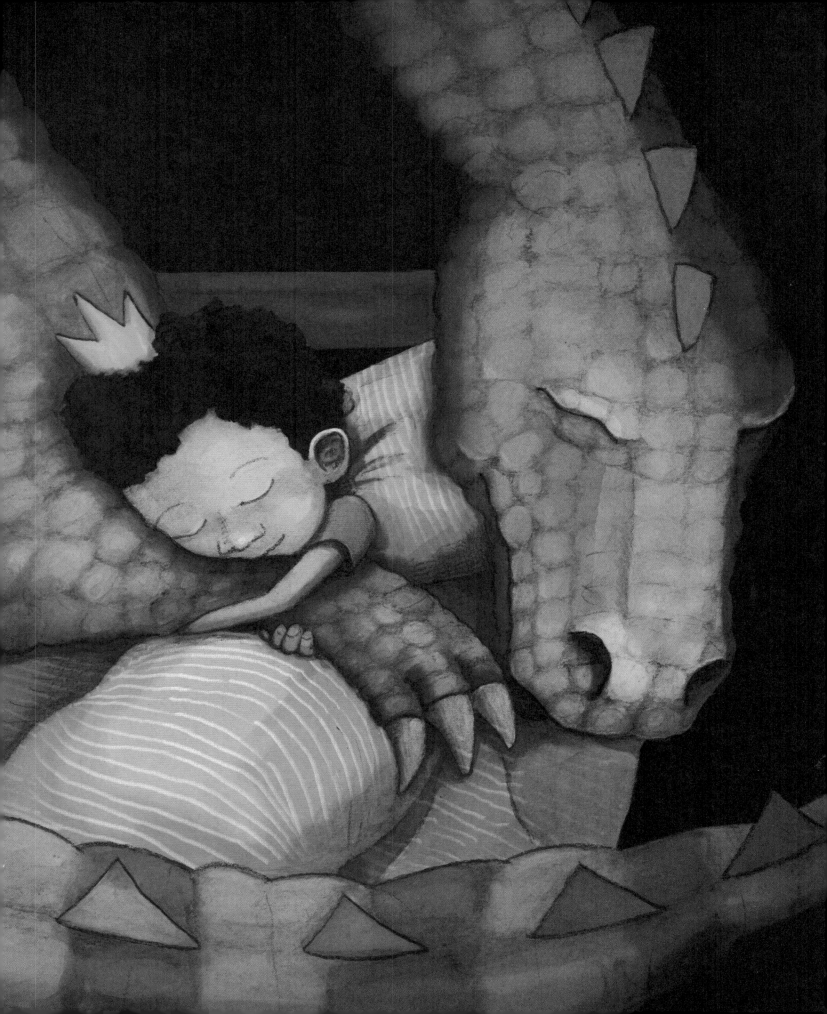

One day the two friends were playing cards.
Prince Zebedee was an excellent cardplayer
and always won.

But not this time.

"I won! Hooray!" cheered Ozzie.
"But you cheated," said the prince.
"Cheated? *Moi?* I would never cheat.
Dragons are very honorable."

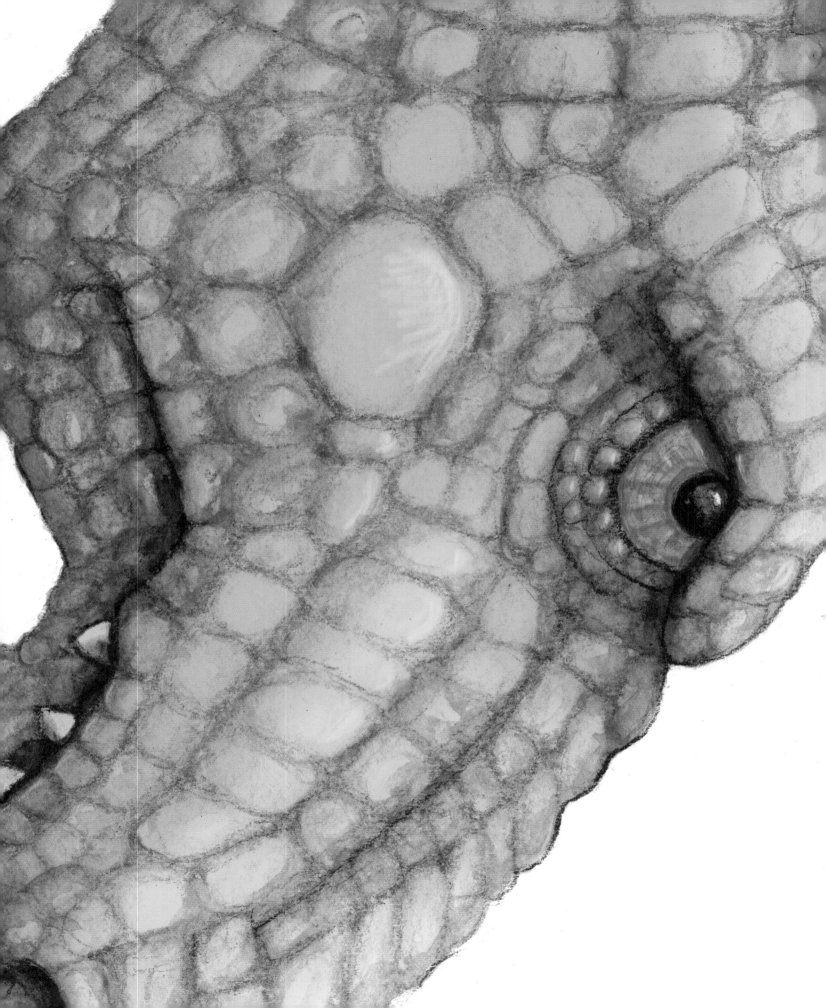

But the argument grew LOUDER and UGLIER.
MEANER and NASTIER.

And when dragons are mad,
sometimes they make bad choices.

GULP!

Finally.

No

more

fighting.

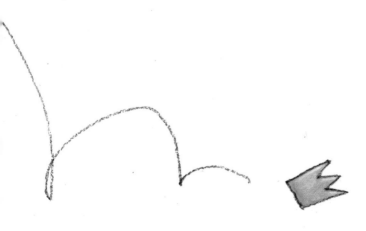

Now Ozzie played all day by himself,
and it wasn't nearly as fun.

And at night his feet were very cold.
He was starting to really miss his best friend.

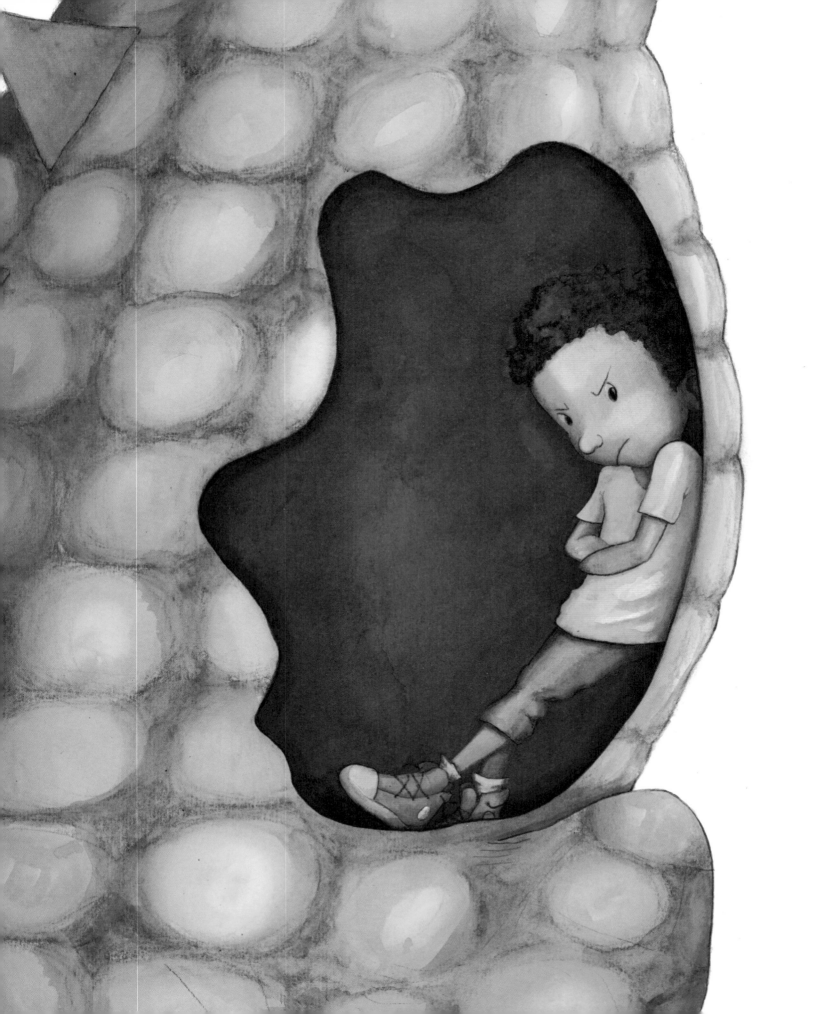

"Are you okay in there, Prince
Zebedee?" asked Ozzie.

"I'm not talking to you, you're
a cheater!" replied the prince.

"GOOD! STAY THERE!
I'm actually having so much fun
without you," said Ozzie.

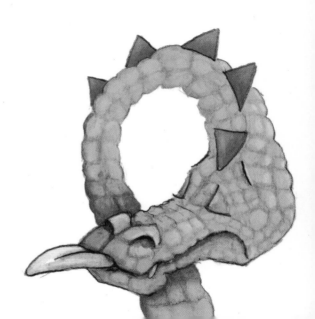

But for an honorable dragon,
Ozzie wasn't being entirely truthful.

He was actually feeling quite lonely.

And sometimes when dragons are lonely,
they make bad choices.

BURP!

Ozzie felt terrible.

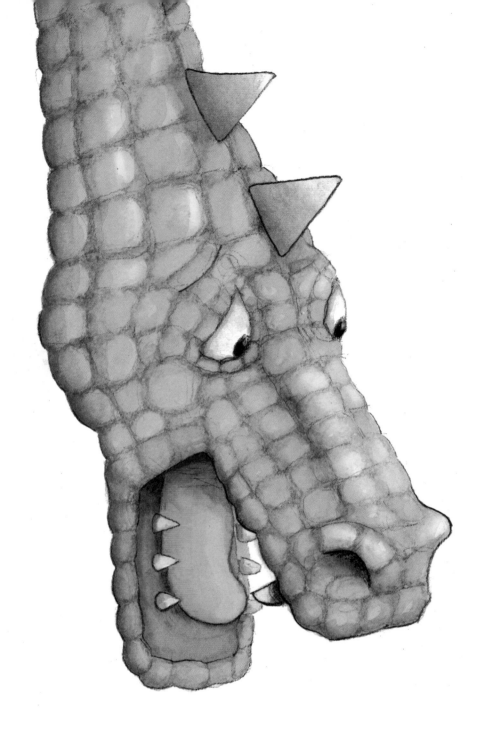

"Zebedee, I miss you! I'm sorry I ate you!"

Deep in Ozzie's belly, Prince Zebedee
heard his friend's apology. "I'm sorry, too.
I shouldn't have called you a cheater,"
Zebedee answered sadly.

And when a prince gets sad, sometimes he cries,
and he cries, and cries, and cries. Which made
Ozzie cry, too.

Slowly, the dragon's belly filled with salty tears.

Until Ozzie **BARFED** up the
whole mess, prince and all.

Ozzie and Prince Zebedee got to work cleaning up.
It felt great to be together again.

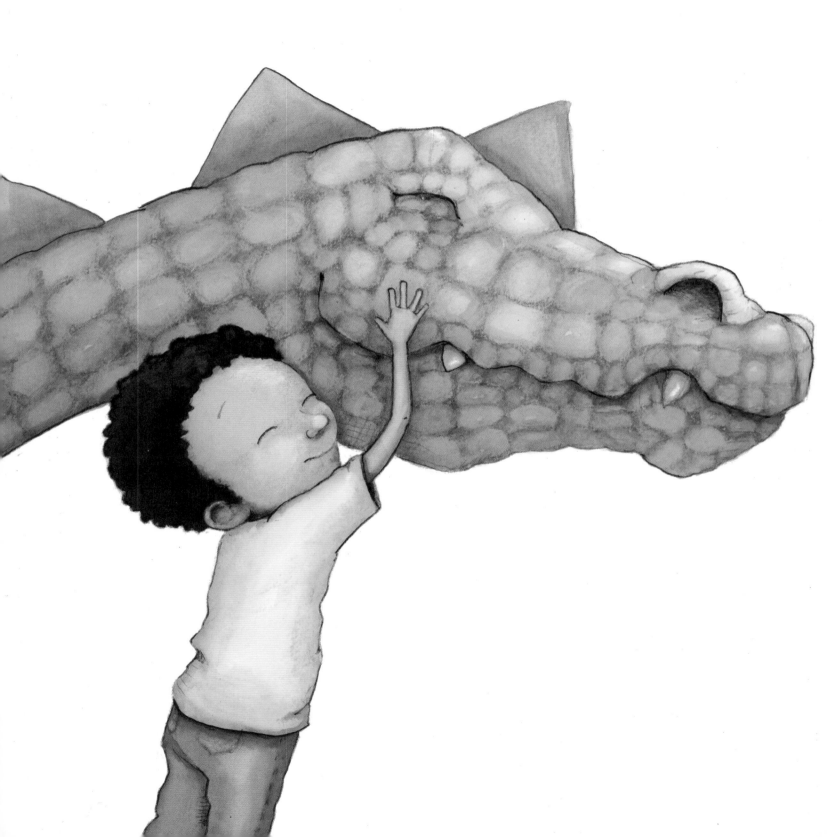

Because they were the best of friends . . .

. . . most times.

To Theo, Eli, and Zoe—for a
lifelong friendship. Don't eat
each other up! —G. K.

FLAMINGO BOOKS
An imprint of Penguin Random House LLC, New York

First published in the United States of America by Flamingo Books,
an imprint of Penguin Random House LLC, 2022

Copyright © 2022 by Gela Kalaitzidis

Flamingo Books & colophon are registered trademarks of Penguin Random House LLC.

Visit us online at penguinrandomhouse.com.

Library of Congress Cataloging-in-Publication Data is available.

Manufactured in China

ISBN 9780593464182

1 3 5 7 9 10 8 6 4 2

H H

Design by Lucia Baez • Text set in Edwardian LT Medium
The artwork for this book was created using watercolor pencils, gouache, and Photoshop.